CW00850827

Written by **Marc Polett** Illustrated by **Vasya Baev**

First edition 2024
Written by Marc Polett
Book design by Vasya Baev

Published in the United States of America
Printed in the United States of America

Hardcover ISBN: 9798989488605
Paperback ISBN: 9798989488612
eBook ISBN: 9798989488629

Dedicated to my wife, Elizabeth, the love of my life and the inspiration for this book.

Special thanks to my Mom and Dad for their love and support.

Once upon a time,
on a warm summer's day
a sweet girl named Lily
went outside to play.

In her bright yellow dress,
she danced in the sun
with plenty of room
to roam and have fun.

While sitting in the
park enjoying a treat,
she spotted a rabbit
with big furry feet.

She followed him closely,
and what did she see?
A hungry squirrel
eating nuts in a tree.

Lily watched them both
with wonder and glee
as a playful dog walked
up to the tree.

The animals looked back,
full of delight

as all four knew
they were friends at first sight!

Benny the rabbit was the softest around
and hopped so high up off the ground.

Lily cuddled him close and tight.
Her arms around him felt just right.

Nutty the squirrel
had a red, bushy tail
and cracked open nuts,
each one without fail.

Lily offered him more,
grinning so bright.
He took them politely,
holding them tight.

Rusty the dog
was a shiny, brown hound
who wagged his tail
when Lily was around.

When she patted his head
with a gentle hand
he felt like the luckiest
dog in the land.

Together they played
in the park so green.
Their love for each other
could clearly be seen.

They ran around
with boundless glee
and laughed out loud,
happy and free.

The four new friends
were having a ball
and promised to play
from summer to fall.

They explored the woods
and the meadows too,
discovering things that
were strange and new.

Benny found
many sweet carrots to crunch.

Nutty found
plenty of acorns to munch.

Rusty led them to
his favorite spot
where they all played
and giggled a lot.

As the day grew old
and the sun began to set,
Lily knew she'd found
her best friends yet.

Together they formed
a beautiful bond
and she knew they'd be friends
forever and beyond!

They said their goodbyes,
wishing to stay,
and promised to return
the very next day!

Lily skipped home
with a heart so light,
knowing her future
was oh-so bright.

That night she slept
with a smile on her face
and dreamed of her friends
and their happy place.

And when she awoke
to a brand-new day,
she knew it would hold
adventure and play.

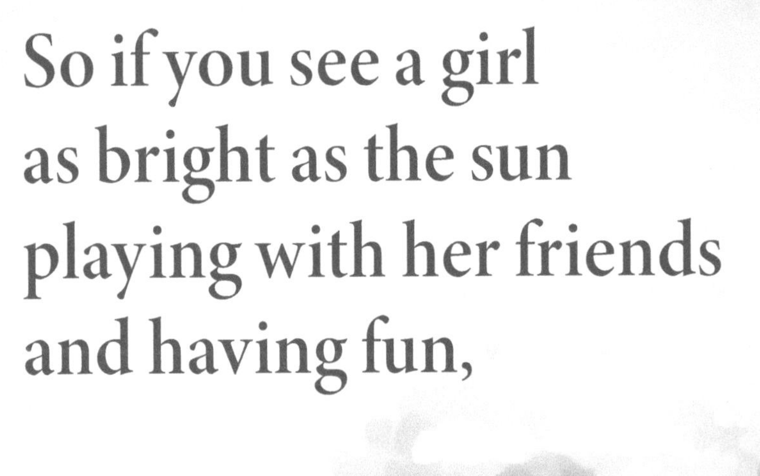

So if you see a girl
as bright as the sun
playing with her friends
and having fun,

give her a smile,
and wave to say hi.
Join in the fun!
No need to be shy!

Lily and her friends
are always here
with love and joy
and laughter and cheer.

The more the merrier, they always say
so join them for a fun-filled day!

Marc Polett loves writing and storytelling and was inspired to write this book by his wife's love of animals and her unique ability to understand them. Marc was born and raised in scenic Gladwyne, PA, and spent his childhood exploring the parks and trails that are spread throughout the historic town, finding peace in nature.
Marc received a bachelor's degree in Sociology from the University of Arizona, where he also studied poetry and creative writing and earned an MBA from Temple University's Fox School of Business. Marc began his career in web development and now works in finance. He has experience in graphic design and mobile game development but has found writing to be his favorite form of creative expression.

Lily's Wondrous World: A Day in the Park is the first story in a four-book series, so stay tuned for the next adventure of Lily and her animal friends.

Vasya Baev is a talented illustrator who defies convention. With a master's degree in computer science and a professional background as a software engineer and graphic designer, Vasya is the founder and Chief Technology Officer of Rockids, an initiative dedicated to nurturing early literacy development.
As an illustrator, Vasya blends his natural artistic abilities with the remarkable potential of generative AI tools like Midjourney and Stable Diffusion. In every one of his illustrations, you'll find a blend of art, technology, and a deep commitment to enriching young minds. You can also see Vasya's work in *Santa's Christmas Dilemma: What to Give Your Animal Friends.*

Printed in the USA
CPSIA information can be obtained
at www.ICGtesting.com
LVHW061342230224
772481LV00002B/2

* 9 7 9 8 9 8 9 4 8 8 6 0 5 *

9 798989 488605